Deep Trouble!

D0337135

EGMONT
We bring stories to life

First published in Great Britain in 2007
by Egmont UK Limited, 239 Kensington High Street, London W8 6SA
© 2007 S4C International Limited and Prism Art & Design Limited, a HIT Entertainment Limited company. All rights reserved.
The Fireman Sam name and character are trademarks of S4C International Limited and Prism Art & Design Limited,
a HIT Entertainment Limited company.

ISBN 978 1 4052 2935 7
3 5 7 9 10 8 6 4 2
Printed in Singapore

In the Fire Station garden, Norman Price and Mandy Flood had come to visit Fireman Sam in his special inventing shed.

"Cor, what's that you've made, Sam?" asked Norman.

"It's a funny-looking spade!" said Mandy.

"It's not a spade, silly! This is my new super-duper beep-o-matic metal detector," said Fireman Sam.

Beep! Beep! Beep! went the beep-o-matic.

"If there's treasure to be found, the beep-o-matic will find it!" smiled Sam.

"Where are you going to try it first?" asked Mandy.

"Pontypandy Mountain is the best place," Sam replied. "Maybe I'll find some buried treasure!"

Just then, Elvis poked his head around the door. "Sam, I've made some of your favourite rock cakes!"

"Coming, Elvis!" said Fireman Sam. "Got to go, kids. Sounds like I'll be taking another trip to the dentist!"

When Sam had gone indoors, Norman ran over to the beep-o-matic metal detector. "Come on Mandy, let's go treasure hunting!"

"Shouldn't we ask Sam first?" worried Mandy.

"Oh, he won't mind. As long as we put it back before he finds out!" said Norman cheekily. He took a coin out of his pocket and held it up. "We might even find some ancient coins!"

That afternoon at the Fire Station, Elvis and Penny were keeping fit.

"We could be in for a storm, soon," said Penny, looking out of the window.

Just then, there was a rumble of thunder in the distance.

"Oh dear, I hope no one is out on Pontypandy Mountain," said Elvis.

"Or Tom might have a few visitors at the Mountain Rescue cabin!" added Penny.

Up on Pontypandy Mountain, Norman and Mandy started their treasure hunt in the middle of an old stone circle.

"Let's try here," said Mandy.

"OK. The treasure will soon be ours!" said Norman, swinging the beep-o-matic metal detector into action.

Beep! Beep! Beep! it went.

"Er, Norman, did you feel that? The ground just went all wobbly!" gasped Mandy.

"Don't worry, that must mean there's treasure down below. Let's get digging!"

Beep! Beep! Beep! went the beep-o-matic metal detector again.

Norman took out his trowel and began to dig, scooping soil over his shoulder.

"Ugh! Careful, Norman. I just got a mouthful of dirt!" said Mandy. "Let me have a go!"

"Here go you. I've got a spare trowel in my rucksack," said Norman.

But as Norman turned around, the ground wobbled and gave way . . . a large hole appeared . . . and Mandy disappeared down it!

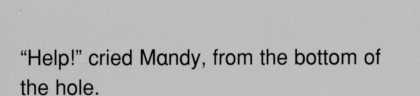

"Help!" cried Mandy, from the bottom of the hole.

"Mandy?" said Norman, spinning round. "Are you all right?"

He shone his torch down the hole, to where Mandy was sitting in the dark.

"I think so," she whimpered. "It's so cold and dark, I can't see a thing."

"Hang on, Mandy," shouted Norman.
"I've got an idea!"

He went to his rucksack and took out a
long rope. He tied one end of the rope
around the torch and lowered it to the
bottom of the hole.

"Got it!" called Mandy. "Thanks, Norman!"

Mandy shone the torch around the cave and to her surprise, she saw a glittering display of treasure.

"Wow!" she shouted. "You'll never guess what I've found!"

But Norman had already gone to fetch help.

Norman ran all the way to the Mountain Rescue Station and before long, he was back at the hole, with Tom Thomas.

"We were digging for treasure when the ground just gobbled Mandy up!" Norman was telling Tom.

"I'm going to need help with this," said Tom. "We'd better call Fireman Sam."

Tom radioed the Fire Station and before long, Fireman Sam and Penny arrived on the scene. The mountain roads were too muddy for Jupiter the fire engine, so they drove there in Penny's car, Venus.

"Let's get Mandy out as quickly as we can, I don't like the look of those storm clouds," said Fireman Sam.

Penny and Tom quickly set up a winch over the hole, while Sam put on his safety harness.

"Right, I'm going in!" said Sam. "Lower me down, nice and slowly."

"Easy does it!" said Fireman Sam.

Mandy was very pleased to see him!

"Don't worry, Mandy," smiled Sam. "There's a cup of hot chocolate waiting for you in Tom's cabin!"

He lifted the harness and fastened it safely around Mandy, then called:

"OK, Tom, pull her up!"

Tom used all his strength to slowly wind the winch, until Mandy was safely back on the ground again. "Phew! You're heavier than you look, Mandy!" he puffed.

Penny wrapped a blanket around Mandy, to keep her warm.

"OK, Sam," shouted Tom. "Your turn now!"

Soon, everyone was safe and sound again.

Back in Tom's Mountain Rescue cabin, everyone warmed up with a cup of hot chocolate.

"You had a lucky escape," Sam said to Mandy. "Of course, none of this would have happened if a certain person hadn't borrowed my beep-o-matic."

"Sorry, Sam," said Norman.

"What I can't understand is why Mandy was so heavy. She's only small," said Tom.

"Maybe it was because of these?" said Mandy. She turned out her pockets and gold coins fell on to the floor.

"Half of the treasure is mine!" shouted Norman.

"Great Fires of London!" said Sam. "This is ancient gold. We'll have to take it to the Pontypandy Museum."

"Oh, no," groaned Norman. "That's the last time I go treasure hunting with you, Mandy Flood!"

Stay Safe!

Can you remember what to do if a fire breaks out?

Get out.
Get the Fire Brigade out.
Stay out!

Sam's Safety Tips

- Never play with matches or lighters.

- If you smell smoke or see fire, tell a grown-up.

- Don't play near hot ovens, or boiling pots and pans.

- Keep toys and clothes away from fires and heaters.

- Ask a grown-up to fit a smoke alarm in your house and test it regularly.